Alfred A. Knopf
New York

DUNCAN THE STORY DRAGON

Amanda
Driscoll

Duncan the Dragon loved to read.

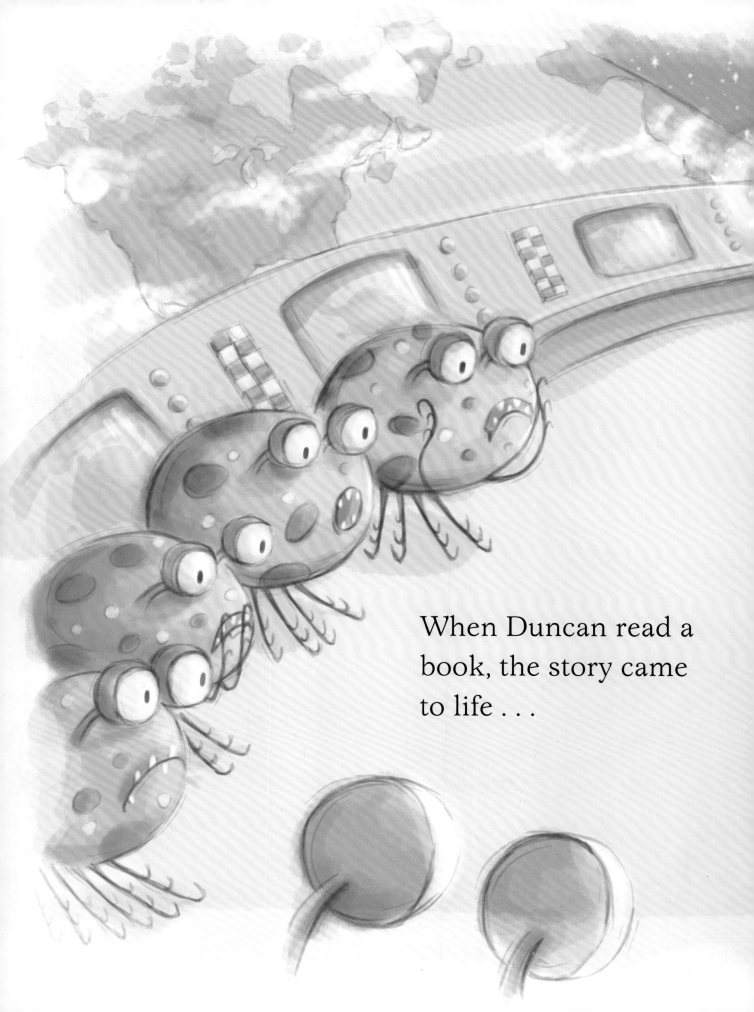

When Duncan read a
book, the story came
to life . . .

and his imagination caught fire.

Unfortunately, so did his book.

"I just want to finish a book," said Duncan.

"I need to know what happens.

Do the pirates find treasure?

Does the captain save the ship?

Do aliens conquer the earth?

"And I want to read those two wonderful words, like the last sip of a chocolate milk shake . . . 'The End.'"

Duncan tried everything to keep his cool.

Really.

Truly.

Everything.

"I have an idea!" said Duncan.
"I will find a friend to read to me."

So Duncan searched a nearby neighborhood.

"Hello, friend," he said to the raccoon. "Would you please read me this book?"

Duncan explored an evergreen forest.

"Hello, friend," he said to
a possum. "Could you
please read me this book?"

Duncan traveled to a faraway farm.

"Hello, friend," he said to the bull. "Will you please read me this book?"

After searching the entire countryside,
Duncan trudged back to his cottage.

As he hugged his book, a fat tear trickled down Duncan's cheek.

It landed with a plop . . .

dribble-drabbled across the floor . . .

then ran split-splat
into a mouse.

"Sad ending?" asked the mouse.
"I'll never know," said Duncan.
As Duncan explained his
problem, he noticed a twinkle
in the mouse's eye.

"Do *you* like books?"
Duncan asked.

"I LOVE books!"
said the mouse.

"Would you . . . could you . . . will you please read me this book?"

"Certainly!" said the mouse.
So the mouse read to Duncan (carefully).

Together they battled
sea monsters . . .

dodged icebergs . . .

. . . and discovered
new lands.

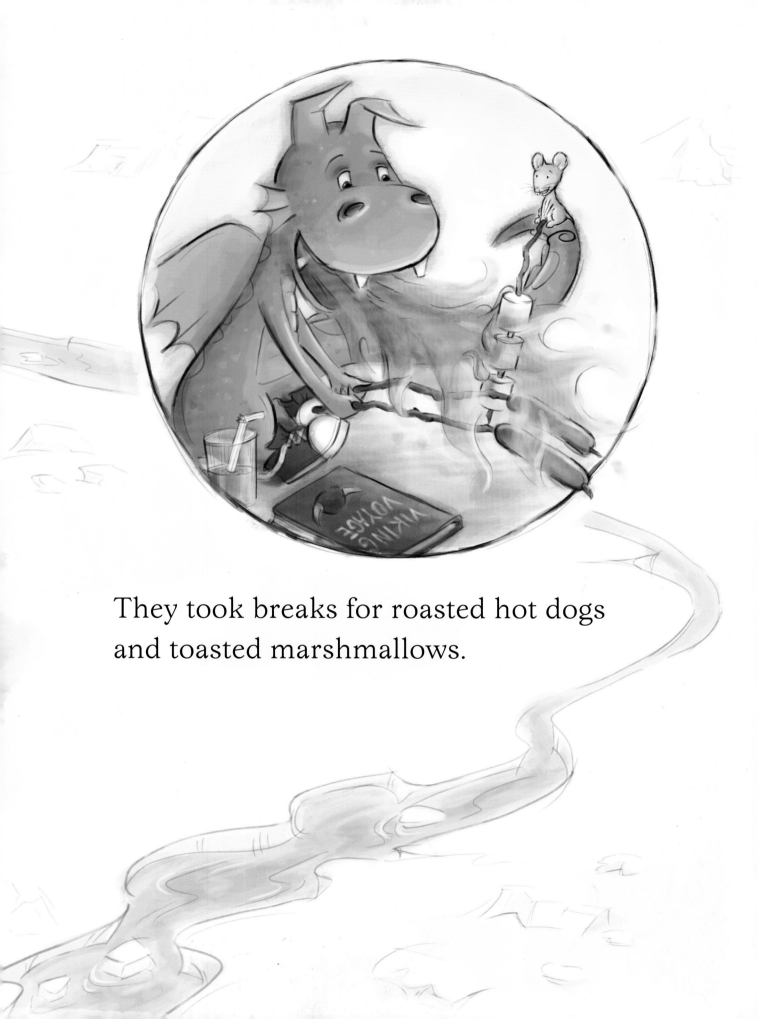

They took breaks for roasted hot dogs
and toasted marshmallows.

Finally, the friends sailed home. Then the mouse read those two wonderful words, like the last sip of a chocolate milk shake . . .

But actually, it was only the beginning.

For Mom and Dad,

with two wonderful words . . .

"love" and "gratitude"

THIS IS A BORZOI BOOK PUBLISHED BY ALFRED A. KNOPF

Copyright © 2015 by Amanda Driscoll

All rights reserved. Published in the United States by Alfred A. Knopf, an imprint of Random House
Children's Books, a division of Random House LLC, a Penguin Random House Company, New York.
Knopf, Borzoi Books, and the colophon are registered trademarks of Random House LLC.

Visit us on the Web! randomhousekids.com
Educators and librarians, for a variety of teaching tools, visit us at RHTeachersLibrarians.com

Library of Congress Cataloging-in-Publication Data
Driscoll, Amanda, author, illustrator.
Duncan the Story Dragon / Amanda Driscoll. — First edition.
p. cm.
ISBN 978-0-385-75507-8 (trade) — ISBN 978-0-385-75508-5 (lib. bdg.) —
ISBN 978-0-385-75509-2 (ebook)
[1. Dragons—Fiction. 2. Books and reading—Fiction. 3. Friendship—Fiction. 4. Animals—Fiction.] I. Title.
PZ7.D7866Du 2015
[E]—dc23
2013049297

The illustrations in this book were created using pencil sketches painted in Adobe Photoshop.

MANUFACTURED IN CHINA
June 2015   10 9 8 7 6 5 4 3 2 1   First Edition